Toby Rogue

By: Frank Waters

Illustrated by: Joyce Bugaiski

Title: Toby Rogue

Edited by Jan George, www.sagewordsservices.com

Cover artwork: Joyce Bugaiski, cover designed by Sage Words Services

A Sage Words Publishing Book
www.sagewordspublishing.com

Sage Words Publishing
ISBN-13: 978-0991501496
ISBN-10: 0991501497

Many years ago in a small English village there was a local riding school by the name of Rowlers. It was a fun place for both children and adults as they gathered to enjoy the horses and ponies. There were about twenty in all ranging from the smallest of Shetland ponies to a 17 h.h. Thoroughbred. Everyone who was crazy about horses loved to gather here and play at being the typical horsey person.

Cary, who had taken the riding school over from her father Ron, ran the everyday business of lessons and supervising the staff. There were two grooms and lots of volunteers. They were always sweeping the yard, cleaning the saddles and bridles and wanting to help all they could. They also helped with every other job around a stable yard. In other words, they were horse mad and loved to come and play at Rowlers.

One of the older ponies who had been at Rowlers for several years was a little Shetland pony. He was full of all the mischief one could imagine. He got his nose into everything and was always in trouble. His name was Toby Rogue and Toby had the run of the yard. He was brown and white which was called a Skewbald. His tail was very long and trailed on the floor and a long mane with a forelock that totally covered his eyes. Toby Rogue looked like a rather large barrel on four little legs and had a very bushy coat. He was always shaking his head at you in a threatening way but he never hurt a soul, even though his eyes, when you could see them, always had a twinkle and gleamed of mischief.

Toby Rogue, who though adorable, was a little monster in his own right. He got into everything he could and was always causing havoc. Toby Rogue loved to squeeze his way into the feed room and knock all the lids off the feed bins, trying to find what he could enjoy to snack on. Often he pushed them over with his head because he was too small to reach over the edges. Of course, this signaled to everyone that he was in the feed room once again. Before he could make an absolute pig of himself, someone always rushed in to save the day.

At night he was locked in his stall, to which he thoroughly objected. For quite a while he would kick his feed bucket around the floor and tip his water over in anger. He would bang on his door with his foot and eventually gave up when he was ignored, Toby Rogue was a rogue indeed. One day when he was out and about, he decided, when nobody was looking, to climb up the step into the tack room. What chaos he caused as he ran around knocking saddles over, pulling bridles off the wall and shaking his head in glee. Once he was caught, Toby Rogue always had a look on his face that said, *Ha, ha, look what I just did*, naughty, naughty Toby Rogue.

One day, Cary decided that Toby Rogue would retire from lessons and the riding school. For years he had carried hundreds of children both in the school and out riding on the country lanes. Funny thing was, he was always a perfect gentlemen when a small child was riding him. Though in the back of his mind, I know it would have given him great pleasure to buck them off right into a ditch or head first into a hedge.

When Cary announced the news that Toby Rogue was retiring, one of her adult students, who had two small children, asked if they could adopt him. Cary was delighted that Toby Rogue would go to a good home. The people who adopted him were called David and Sally McDonald and their children were Sara and Peter. Sara and Peter could not be more delighted that they soon would be the proud owners of their very own pony. Little did they know what adventures they were in for and about to encounter. Sara was five years old and Peter was almost eight, just the right age for a Shetland pony.

One week later, Mrs. McDonald had arranged with Cary to collect Toby Rogue from Rowlers Riding School. The McDonalds had a charming house about five miles away which stood on four acres of ground. Plenty of room for Toby Rogue to roam around and play with the children. Mr. McDonald had spent the week building a stable for Toby Rogue. It was situated by the gate of the paddock where their little friend would live. Little did they know the tricks that this little monkey of a pony would get up to and the havoc he would cause. He was about to really live up to his name, Toby Rogue.

Mrs. McDonald backed the trailer into the stable yard and Sara very excitedly came out with a brand new halter they had bought for Toby Rogue. Today was the day their new little friend was to be moved the five miles to his new home. The McDonalds had hired the trailer to transport Toby Rogue to the four acres that would now be his new home. Of course, at first, being Toby Rogue, he would not go into the trailer. Not that he was afraid, he just wanted to show them WHO was boss. Cary knew how to get him up the ramp. She got a very large carrot and allowed Toby Rogue to bite a little off the end. Of course, that did it, Toby Rogue wanted the rest of that large carrot and when Cary walked up into the trailer, he shot off like a rocket after her and snatched the rest of the carrot out of her hand. One thing we can say about Toby Rogue, he was no dummy and knew exactly what he wanted, especially when it came to food.

The ramp was raised and locked as they set off on the five-mile journey to Toby Rogue's new home. Sara and Peter were full of excitement and had already told all their friends that they had a new pony on the way. They had many adventures planned with their friends and Toby Rogue. However, they could not have known WHO would be totally in charge of these plans! They were going to have their hands full more than they EVER dreamed possible.

On arrival at home, Sara and Peter could not wait to lower the ramp. To their surprise, as the ramp came down, they discovered that Toby Rogue had already slipped out of his halter and was loose in the trailer. He bolted down the ramp past them with his tail high in the air. He galloped right around the back of the house. Right there in front of him was a line of clean clothing, that had just been washed, wafting in the breeze. Toby Rogue did not care and shot straight through the middle, braking the washing line and dragging sheets, shirts, towels, and many other things with him. One of the sheets totally covered him and he looked like a ghost pony. Both Sara and Peter fell on the floor and could not stop laughing. Of course, Mrs. McDonald was not at all pleased and was frantically running around picking up her washing off the ground that was now all dirty again.

When Toby Rogue realized that he wasn't being chased, he stopped dead. Still covered in the sheet, he put his head down and started to eat the lush grass of the garden. The pony had left some heavy hoof marks all around the lawn. Mrs. McDonald knew that her husband David would not be very pleased when he saw his lawn. After Toby Rogue had totally filled his mouth to capacity with grass, he looked over at Mrs. McDonald, Sara and Peter. He shook his head up and down with a look on his face that said, how did you like that then? He then shook off the sheet and turned around walking toward Peter and Sara and in the process, walked right over the sheet. Mrs. McDonald was not amused and already thinking, *Oh my, what in Heavens name have we done?* Once she realized that Toby Rogue was making his own way to the children, she waited to see if he would allow Sara to put on the halter and he let her, she led him to his new stable.

Mrs. McDonald was still angry and asked the children to close the door and put the bolt on from the outside. Toby Rogue did not like this at all and let everyone know by constantly banging on the inside of the door with his foot. He then proceeded to knock over his water bucket and kick it all around his stable. Cary Rowler had already told Mr. McDonald to put the bolt down around the middle of the door so that Toby Rogue could not reach it. Toby Rogue absolutely knew how to slide it back and push open the door. Of this he was a total expert and had opened many doors throughout his life at Rowlers.

When Mr. McDonald came home, Mrs. McDonald took the trailer back to the rental agency. In the back of her mind she was thinking, *shall I keep it just in case we have to take this little bundle of mischief back to Rowlers?* She knew in her heart though that this would be an enormous disappointment to the children and somehow realized that Toby Rogue would be here to stay. The next day, the children were driven to school and Toby Rogue was left out grazing in the paddock with the gate closed. Mrs. McDonald decided on her return from school to bake some apple pies. When they were taken out of the oven, she sprinkled them with sugar and left them on the kitchen counter top to cool. She then decided to go upstairs, make the beds and do the rest of the chores.

Suddenly, on the breeze, Toby Rogue got a whiff of the apple pies coming through the kitchen window and knowing how to open a gate, he did just that. He decided to make his way to the wonderful aroma coming from the house.

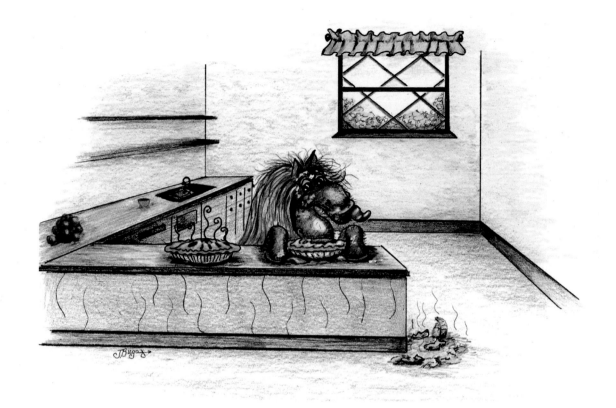

He trotted across the lawn and through the door to the kitchen which Mrs. McDonald had left open and sure enough, right in front of him were THE APPLE PIES! It did not take him long to shove his nose into the pie closest to him. This was one of three that Mrs. McDonald had baked and as his nose hit it, the plate crashed to the floor sending pie EVERYWHERE!

Naturally, this made a loud breaking noise that alerted Mrs. McDonald. She ran quickly down the stairs. To see Toby Rogue, in the kitchen, already eating the second pie that was still on the counter.

She screamed at him, in horror, to which he just turned his head and shook it at her. She took one look and burst out laughing. Toby Rogue's muzzle, face, eye lashes, forelock and whiskers were totally caked in pastry, apple, juice and sugar. He merely continued to munch away at the pie.

Mrs. McDonald sat down in a chair and laughed for about five minutes. Toby Rogue just ignored her and continued to eat the apple pie to his heart's content. He chased a plate across the counter and was standing right in the middle of the one he had knocked on the floor. His feet looked like they had just come out of the oven, covered in pastry and apple.

Mrs. McDonald managed to get hold of his forelock to which Toby Rogue totally objected. However, she held firm and led him back to his stable, put him inside and bolted the door. He was NOT happy about this and proceeded to kick the inside quickly and LOUDLY as Mrs. McDonald walked back to the kitchen to clean up. Of course, she closed and locked the back door this time having now learned her lesson not to leave doors open when Toby Rogue was not secure in his stable. When Sara and Peter came home from school and she told them what had happened, they all sat on the floor and laughed and laughed. Mrs. McDonald was only sad that she had not taken pictures of Toby Rogue for the family album as this was an absolute first for them and a classic. However, little did she know that in the future she would have many more opportunities to take photographs of Toby Rogue's mischief and antics.

The children had invited a couple of friends over to have a little ride on Toby Rogue and they had bought a used saddle and bridle from Cary Rowler. They were excited, as this was to be their first ride on him since he arrived the day before and what better way than to share it with friends. Gary and Emily Talbert-Smith arrived as planned, wearing their jodhpurs and looked very smart as did Sara and Peter. They walked down to the stable and Toby Rogue was standing with his head to the back of the stable sulking.

He had been in there now for about four hours and he did not like it at all. As they opened the door, he turned around, looked at them, shook his head up and down and bolted out of the door into the paddock, past the children. Fortunately, they had closed the gate but he was determined that he would not be caught. The closer they got, the further he ran away. Sara put a plan together and all four held hands and slowly drove Toby Rogue into a corner so that he could not escape. They surrounded him and Peter put the halter rope around Toby Rogue's neck and led him back into his stable. They closed the door so that he could not bolt again and tacked him up with his saddle and bridle.

Guess what? He would not come out and planted his feet firmly on the ground of his stable. Peter remembered the trick of Cary's getting him into the trailer. He got a carrot and waved it in front of Toby Rogue's nose. Magically that did the trick and he followed Peter out of his stable and into the paddock. While Toby Rogue ate a little of the carrot, Sara climbed into the saddle, kicked him on and trotted around the paddock. The children cheered with glee that they were at home riding their very own pony. Mrs. McDonald came out to watch and Toby Rogue gave her one of his mischievous looks as much as to say, *I want more apple pie so you had better not leave*

that back door open again. Mrs. McDonald knew what he was thinking and smiled.

All the children took turns riding Toby Rogue and he behaved like a perfect gentleman while they rode him. Mrs. McDonald felt totally comfortable that once the children were sitting on his back, they were quite safe.

At the end of the day, a very tired but content Peter and Sara said goodnight to Gary and Emily. They bedded Toby Rogue down for the night, fed him and filled his water bucket. In spite of his mischief and roguish ways, they both hugged him goodnight and bolted his stable door. As they headed toward the house for dinner and bedtime, they both looked back toward the stable and noticed the silence. Toby Rogue was not banging the door with his foot anymore. They climbed into their beds that night as happy as two children could ever be and wondered what the next adventures would be with their new little bundle of mischief at the bottom of the garden, Toby Rogue.

Frank Waters is a former show jumping rider from Great Britain who retired from competition in 1972 and became a show jumping commentator. This led to many events and he moved to the United States in 1980 continuing his career announcing. He now announces every discipline including Jumpers/Hunters/Dressage/ Breeds and even some Western. His biggest accomplishments to date include the Asian Games and the Pan Arab Games in the Middle East. Frank wrote his first book to great success which was published one year ago by Sage Words Publishing, www.sagewordspublishing.com and has become a wonderful success story. Now he has ventured into the world of writing for children with Toby Rogue, please enjoy this fun book and thank you to my good friend Joyce for the wonderful illustrations.

Joyce Bugaiski was born in Washington DC and lived in S.E. DC until the age of 19 when she moved to Florida. She was a very poor child and had very few toys so her imagination was always working overtime and she created a wonderful world of make believe for herself.

Joyce wasn't always an artist which is what she tells the children that she encounters. She didn't begin to draw or paint until she was in her somewhat senior years. So, she tells them, "no matter what you want in life, go for it, work for it. You can be anything you want to be if you want it in your heart." Always follow your heart.

Her family, her heritage and her art is what keeps her heart happy and her spirit healthy. Her art, both two and three dimensional is done out of vision and love. Vision of what she sees with her eyes and love of what she feels with her heart. She tries to draw what brings peace and joy to herself and to others. Her art reflects her heritage, traditional values and what gives her joy. She tries to spread joy and kindness wherever she can and encourage the younger generation to be kind regardless of anyone else's circumstance.

Made in the USA
Monee, IL
11 November 2022

17536627R00024